D.J.'S BACK FROM SPAIN WITH A SURPRISE!

"D.J., where's the big surprise?" Michelle interrupted. She was jumping up and down with excitement.

"Oh, right," said D.J., smiling. "It's a surprise that all of you will like . . . a lot."

"Is it a trip to Magic Mountain?" asked Michelle.

D.J. shook her head. Then she turned to the boy who stood next to her. "Everyone, this is Steve. And Steve, this is my dad, my uncle Jesse, Becky, and Joey. And these are my little sisters, Stephanie and Michelle."

Michelle looked as devastated as Stephanie felt. The little girl stepped closer to Steve. "Excuse me. Let me get this straight. You're the surprise?"

FULL HOUSE

Take a Hike, Romeo

by Wendy Wax

Based on the series FULL HOUSE™ created by
Jeff Franklin

and on episodes written by
Jay Abramowitz
Tom Burkhard
Marc Warren & Dennis Rinsler

A PARACHUTE PRESS BOOK

Parachute Press, Inc.
156 Fifth Avenue
New York, NY 10010

ISBN: 0-938753-75-4
Printed in the United States of America
April 1993
10 9 8 7 6 5 4 3 2 1

ONE

"**Dad!**" Stephanie Tanner called up the living room stairs. If she had to wait one more minute, she would explode. She stomped over to the kitchen door. "Uncle Jesse! Aunt Becky! Joey!" she yelled. "We have to leave now! We can't be late!"

"Late for what?" asked six-year-old Michelle, who had just come inside from playing with a friend.

"For the airport, silly," Stephanie reminded

1

her younger sister. "How could you forget that D.J.'s coming home from Spain today? She's only been gone for two whole months."

"All right!" cried Michelle. "Dad! Uncle Jesse! Come on. Let's go."

Michelle might have forgotten that their older sister was due home today, but Stephanie had been counting the days. With D.J. away on a high school foreign-study program with her best friend Kimmy Gibbler, it had been a miserable summer. Stephanie, who was almost eleven, had been stuck going to this stupid day camp, which she liked to call Camp Day o' Fun. Her father had made her go, even though she'd told him a million times how humiliating it was to be the oldest camper there.

Stephanie couldn't wait to tell D.J. all about it. D.J. would understand why she'd hated camp. D.J. knew that Stephanie wasn't a kid anymore.

"Hey, girls," said their uncle Jesse as he

came into the living room from the kitchen. "Can we have some peace and quiet around here?" He was carrying two toddler-size cups of juice. "Nicky and Alex are still napping."

Nicky and Alex were Uncle Jesse and Aunt Becky's two-year-old twins. When the Tanner girls' mother died several years ago in a car accident, Uncle Jesse and his best friend Joey had moved in to give the girls' dad a hand. Since then Jesse had married Becky, and they'd had the boys. Now the four of them lived upstairs in the attic, while Joey's room was downstairs in the basement. With such a crowded house, there was always something happening. D.J., Stephanie, and Michelle usually loved every minute of it—unless, of course, one of them wanted some privacy!

"But Uncle Jesse," Stephanie said, "if Nicky and Alex are going to the airport with us, they have to wake up anyway."

"Don't worry, Stef," Uncle Jesse reassured her as he tightened the lids on the cups of juice and stuck the cups in a big blue bag. "Becky and I are taking our own car. We're dropping off the boys at Aunt Ida's house before we go to the airport." When he said "Aunt Ida," he made a face.

Stephanie giggled. Aunt Ida was related to Becky, and she and Jesse didn't get along very well. Aunt Ida disapproved of Jesse's long hair, his motorcycle, and especially his band, Jesse and the Rippers.

They heard footsteps behind the kitchen door, and then Joey entered the room. "I'm ready," he said.

"I like your hat, Joey," Stephanie said. "But I don't get it."

Joey was wearing a baseball cap with a lit-up sign that said WE COME BACK, D.J.

He took off the cap and peered at it. "Oh. It's supposed to read 'Welcome back, D.J.' I guess the l is missing." He shrugged. "D.J. will get the idea," he said in his best Popeye voice. "She knows we're happy to have her home."

4

Joey could imitate all sorts of voices. In fact, he once had his own TV comedy show for kids. Now Joey and Jesse had their own radio show, so Joey had the chance to practice different voices all day long.

"Do you know what's taking Dad so long?" Stephanie asked with a sigh. "We're never going to get out of here. I want to be at the airport when D.J. steps off the plane."

"He's on the phone with Vicky," Joey said.

"Oh, no." Stephanie and Michelle looked at each other and groaned at the same time. It wasn't that they didn't like their dad's girlfriend, Vicky. Actually, they liked her a lot. But Vicky lived in Chicago and they lived in San Francisco. That meant a long-distance relationship, which meant lots of long-distance phone calls, which meant they were going to be waiting for their father, Danny, a long time. They'd never make it to the airport on time.

Danny had met Vicky on the set of his morning television show, *Wake Up, San*

Francisco. Vicky had been filling in as co-anchor for Becky while Becky was on maternity leave with the twins. When Becky returned to work, Vicky accepted another TV host job in Chicago. Danny missed her a lot.

Stephanie plopped down onto the couch and rested her chin on her hands. She heaved a sigh of relief when Becky came into the living room carrying a twin in each arm. As usual, they looked totally adorable. Today their hair was plastered straight back, and they each wore tiny blue jeans and a T-shirt. Nicky's T-shirt was blue and Alex's was yellow. "Okay, the boys are ready," Becky said.

"For what? The Eddie Munster look-alike contest?" asked Jesse, messing up his sons' hair. He liked them to wear it long and loose, the same way he did.

"You know what my aunt Ida says," said Becky. "With their hair in their eyes she can never see their faces."

6

"Yeah," remarked Jesse, "but on the plus side, they can never see hers."

Becky smacked him playfully.

Stephanie couldn't sit still for another second. She jumped to her feet and began pacing up and down the living room. She knew calling her father one more time wouldn't do any good. Instead she forced herself to think about all the good things she and D.J. would be doing together soon—getting ready for school, swapping jewelry, hanging out at the mall. . . .

Suddenly something in the pile of mail near the door caught Stephanie's eye. It was a postcard from D.J. Stephanie picked it up and looked at it. On the front was a cute boy wearing a bullfighter's outfit. She turned it over and began to read.

Dear Everyone:

I can't believe that summer's almost over and I'll be home soon. I'm trying not to think too much about going back to school—it's a major drag after my fabulous summer in Europe.

I can't wait to see all of you. I have a really great surprise!

Hasta luego,

D.J.

"This is great," Stephanie announced to the others. "There's a postcard from D.J. here, and she says she has a surprise for us."

Michelle looked excited. "Maybe it's a present," she said eagerly.

Stephanie scanned the postcard again. "She doesn't say, but that's got to be it."

What would D.J. be bringing home from Europe? Stephanie wondered. Maybe she'd have something sophisticated and interesting for Stephanie—like a cool pair of earrings or a Spanish dress that she could wear on the first day of school. Maybe it was a new wallet. . . . Hadn't D.J. told her that you could get really great leather goods in Spain?

Stephanie was so lost in her thoughts

about D.J.'s surprise that she didn't hear Danny come downstairs.

"Come on, everybody," he said impatiently. "Let's get a move on. Do you want to keep D.J. waiting all day?"

Ordinarily Stephanie wouldn't let her father get away with his idea of a joke. But today she was too excited to give him a hard time about anything. In just one more hour, D.J. would finally be home!

TWO

"It says here that D.J.'s plane has just arrived and it's at gate eight," Danny said as he gazed up at one of the airport TV monitors. "Come on, guys and girls—we have no time to lose."

They all bolted down the wide corridor in the direction of the gates, dodging airport workers, travelers carrying luggage, and electric carts.

Just as they reached gate 8, passengers

from the plane began pouring into the waiting-room area. Stephanie looked around and saw that a lot of people were there to meet friends and relatives who'd been to Spain. Many passengers were wearing or carrying souvenirs—castanets, colorful bags, and painted jewelry.

"I can't wait to see the surprise that D.J. is bringing," said Michelle. She was holding Stephanie's hand.

"Yeah," agreed Stephanie. "I hope we have enough room in the car for all her luggage plus this surprise—whatever it is."

Suddenly Stephanie and Michelle spotted D.J.'s best friend, Kimmy Gibbler, coming toward them. She was carrying more souvenirs than almost any other passenger and was wearing a brightly colored flamenco dress. As usual, she was grinning from ear to ear.

"Los Tanneritos! Mi familia!" she cried as she rushed toward them with open arms. She started hugging everyone.

Stephanie didn't want to admit it, but it was good to see Kimmy. She had sort of missed having Kimmy around to argue with. Everyone else was happy to see her, too, even though she tended to get on their nerves—especially Danny's—when she was around every day.

"Kimmy, where is *su familia?*" asked Danny. Kimmy's family never seemed to be around.

"My family?" said Kimmy. "They said to come home with you. I figured you'd be going out for a fancy dinner and you'd treat me."

"Where's D.J.?" Stephanie asked Kimmy impatiently.

"She's right behind me," said Kimmy.

Danny craned his neck, trying to scan the crowd. "I can't see past Romeo and Juliet," he complained. He was talking about a boy and girl who were kissing as other passengers continued to pour into the terminal around them. The boy was tall with dark brown hair, and the girl had long blond hair. Finally the young couple broke apart and looked around.

"That girl looks just like D.J.," said Michelle.

The others gasped. Stephanie couldn't believe it. The girl who had been kissing the boy *was* D.J.!

THREE

When D.J. spotted her family and Kimmy, she rushed over.

"Hi, everyone!" she said with a big smile.

"D.J.!" shouted Michelle.

"You're back!" said Uncle Jesse.

"Hi, Deej." Joey grinned.

"It's great to see you," said Becky.

Everyone said something except Stephanie and Danny. Both of them just stared at D.J. Her skin was tanned and glowing and her

15

eyes were sparkling. She had on jeans, an embroidered blouse, and a new pair of boots. Stephanie had never seen her sister look so confident and grown up. She almost seemed like a stranger.

"Hi, Dad." D.J. gave her father a big hug. "Aren't you going to say hello?"

"Er . . . hi . . . honey," Danny fumbled. "I'm just in shock—that's all."

"D.J., where's the big surprise?" Michelle interrupted. She was jumping up and down with excitement.

"Oh, right," said D.J., smiling. "It's a surprise that all of you will like . . . a lot."

"Is it a trip to Magic Mountain?" asked Michelle.

D.J. shook her head. Then she turned to the boy who stood next to her. "Everyone, this is Steve. And Steve, this is my dad, my uncle Jesse, Becky, and Joey. And these are my little sisters, Stephanie and Michelle."

Little! At that, Stephanie snapped out of the daze she'd been in since D.J. arrived.

Michelle could be considered little, but Stephanie was almost eleven. She was practically a teenager!

"I've heard a lot about you two," said Steve. "I even helped D.J. pick out stuffed animals for both of you," he added, trying to be friendly.

Stuffed animals! Now Stephanie was furious. Stuffed animals were for little girls like Michelle. Didn't D.J. know that she'd given them up last year?

Michelle looked as devastated as Stephanie felt. The little girl stepped closer to Steve. "Excuse me. Let me get this straight. You're the surprise?" She pointed at his face.

D.J. bent down. "Yes, Michelle. Steve and I are going together."

"It's now official," moaned Stephanie. "This has been the worst summer I've ever had." She knew she was being rude, but she couldn't help it. How could her own sister actually think she and Michelle would be excited about this boyfriend of D.J.'s when

17

they were expecting presents?

No one said a word to Steve. Finally Joey offered his hand. "Welcome to the family, son," he said in a Bullwinkle voice. They started to shake hands, but Danny stepped between them.

"Excuse me," Danny began, glaring at Joey. "What exactly do you mean by 'going together,' D.J.?"

"Come on, Mr. T.," interrupted Kimmy. "You're not that old. It means they're like boyfriend and girlfriend."

"*Silencio, el* big mouth," D.J. said, giving Kimmy a look of warning. As usual, Kimmy was about to make a bad situation worse.

"Sorry, Deej," said Kimmy. "*Adios*—I have to get my baggage. I'll meet you down there." Kimmy started off toward the baggage claim area. Then she turned around and called back to them, "I'm looking forward to that lobster dinner!"

"There isn't going to be any lobster dinner!" replied Danny.

Stephanie couldn't resist the perfect opportunity. "That means we'll be dropping you off at home, Gibbler," she said.

Everybody watched Kimmy walk away without saying anything.

"Actually, Dad," said D.J., "you've met Steve before. We went out a couple of times last year. Uncle Jesse, you drove us to the movies once, and Joey, you gave us tickets to that comedy show. Remember?"

"Funny, but I don't recall you mentioning that Steve was going to Spain with you," said Danny.

"I didn't even know he'd be in the foreign-study program until we saw each other on the flight over there," said D.J. Then she and Steve looked dreamily into each other's eyes, remembering that day two months ago.

"*Nunca olvidare ese momento,*" D.J. said in Spanish. In English that meant "I'll never forget that moment."

"*Soy el hombre más contento del mundo,*" Steve answered, holding her hand. "I am the happiest guy in the world."

"En inglés, por favor," said Danny. "Please speak in English."

"Uh, Deej," said Steve awkwardly, "I told my folks I'd meet them at the baggage claim. I'll catch you down there." He backed away and then added nervously, "Great seeing you all again."

"Take a hike, Romeo," Stephanie muttered as Steve walked off quickly in the same direction Kimmy had headed a few minutes before.

"I can't believe this," D.J. said to her dad. "You were so rude to Steve. You're treating me like a child."

"Well, you're not acting like an adult," said Danny. "Making out in the international terminal of a huge airport—what'll people think of America?"

"Dad," said D.J., "I'm sixteen years old."

"I don't care how old you are," said Danny. "That's inappropriate behavior."

"I just spent a whole summer on my

own," D.J. snapped. "Now I wish Steve and I had just stayed in Spain!"

Danny looked around him. "Uh, everybody," he said, "could D.J. and I have a minute?"

"Sure," said the others. No one moved.

"Alone," Danny added.

"*I* want a minute with D.J.," said Michelle.

"Come on, Michelle," said Stephanie, whirling around. "D.J. doesn't want to talk to us *little* sisters."

"Stef . . ." said D.J. "I do too want to talk to you."

But Stephanie and Michelle were already on their way over to the ice cream stand with the others. Joey was going to treat everyone to double-scoop cones.

"Dad, how could you embarrass me in front of Steve like that?" D.J. wailed as she dropped down into one of the waiting-room seats.

"I'm sorry, honey," Danny said. "It's just

that I missed you so much . . . I guess I thought you'd want to run over and give *me* a kiss—not Steve."

"Maybe I should've prepared you a little more for Steve," said D.J.

"It would have helped," admitted Danny. "I mean, I knew you'd probably date some guys in Spain, but I was hoping you'd leave them there."

"Dad, Steve's a great guy," D.J. said, her eyes lighting up. "He's a senior, he's on the wrestling team, he recycles everything." She knew the recycling bit would impress her dad.

"I'm sure he's wonderful," said Danny, "but I want to hear about you and your trip."

D.J. stood and gave Danny a big hug. "Tell you what. When we get home we'll have a cup of coffee, and I'll tell you all about my trip."

"Well, that'll be nice, honey, we can . . . Coffee? Since when do *you* drink coffee?"

"Actually, what I like to drink is *café con leche*," said D.J. "Coffee with milk."

"In this country children don't drink *café con leche*," Danny said. "They drink chocolate milk."

"Dad!" D.J. practically shrieked. "How many times do I have to tell you? I'm sixteen. I've been to Europe. I'm planning on getting a part-time job this semester. I think I'm old enough to choose my own beverage."

"Well, we'll have to talk about that part-time job," said Danny. "Your grades come first. And I didn't choose my own beverage till I was twenty-one," he added as they walked toward the others, "and even then I chose chocolate milk."

"Dad, that is so provincial," said D.J.

"Provincial?" echoed Danny. Since when did D.J. use big words like that? he thought. He had a feeling that having his oldest daughter home from Spain was going to take a lot more getting used to than he'd ever imagined.

FOUR

"Why are you giving the princess blue skin?" Stephanie asked Michelle, who was coloring at the kitchen table. Stephanie pulled out a chair, placed a notebook on the table, and sat down.

"I can color the princess any way I want to," said Michelle. "It's not your coloring book anymore."

"I'm too old for coloring books," Stephanie reminded her. She opened her notebook. "I have to do homework for English class anyway." She sighed. "It's so unfair. We just started school, and my teacher's already making us write a five-page short story."

"What's your story going to be about?" asked Danny. He took some hamburger meat out of the refrigerator and handed it to Becky. The two of them were making dinner.

"I don't know yet," said Stephanie. "That's my problem."

"Why don't you write about summer camp?" said Becky.

Stephanie made a face. "Camp Day o' Fun is the last thing I want to write about," she said.

"Why don't you write about Pigaro and Eduardo?" Michelle pointed across the table to two stuffed animals.

Stephanie glared at the pig D.J. had brought her from Spain. "Michelle, I said you can keep Pigaro only if he stays on your side of our room. I don't want to see him

in the kitchen, the living room, or any-
where else in the house." Why couldn't D.J.
have gotten her a leather belt like the one
she'd brought Becky? Every time Stephanie
saw that stupid pig, she remembered how
D.J. had called her a little kid.

"Watch what you say," said Michelle, cov-
ering the pig's ears. "I just wanted him to
get one last look at the kitchen." She un-
covered the pig's ears. "I like Pigaro the pig
just as much as I like Eduardo the mouse."

"Well, I don't like either of them!" Stephanie snapped. "Stuffed animals are for
babies."

"I'm *not* a baby," said Michelle.

"*I* know you're not, but D.J. thinks we
both are. Haven't you noticed that D.J.'s
been ignoring us ever since she got home?
All she cares about is spending time with
her Romeo."

At that, Danny raised his eyebrows, but
he didn't say anything.

It was true, Stephanie told herself. D.J.

had been home a week, and not a day went by when she didn't see Steve. He came over every morning for breakfast. He walked D.J. home from school every day. Then the two of them did their homework together in the Tanners' living room until Steve had to leave for wrestling practice. And whenever they weren't together, they were talking on the phone. Even Kimmy—who was D.J.'s best friend—hadn't been around very much. D.J. only had time for Steve.

The worst part was that D.J. seemed totally unaware that anything was wrong. The day after she got home, Stephanie had asked her when she wanted to go school shopping, and D.J. had said that she'd already made plans with Steve for the next five days. And then, over the weekend, Michelle had asked D.J. to take her outside to play with her new ball. D.J. had smiled dreamily. "Oh, hi, Michelle," she'd murmured. "Did you say you're going to the mall? Have fun." Then she'd gone back to doodling little hearts around her initials and Steve's.

The truth was, Stephanie realized with a sigh, D.J. didn't know that anyone but Steve was alive. She looked down at the blank page of her notebook again. D.J. had always gotten straight A's in English and had even had Stephanie's teacher. If D.J. were here now, she'd probably know exactly what to write about.

Michelle noticed Stephanie's upset expression.

"Do you need help, Stef?" she asked sweetly. "I'm good at homework."

"No, thanks, Michelle," Stephanie replied. "I have to write a short story, and although you are short, you can't write, so you can't help."

"I can write *i*'s and *t*'s," Michelle said proudly.

"Great story," said Stephanie. "It it it it it."

"Nobody ever lets me help," Michelle complained.

"You can help set the table, honey," said Danny.

"Or you can help mash the potatoes," said Becky.

"I want to mash potatoes!" said Michelle, jumping out of her seat.

Danny shook his head. "One of my favorite household jobs is setting the table," he said. "It's too bad none of my daughters takes after me. It would be so nice to have someone to share it with. Stef?"

"I'm working, Dad," said Stephanie. She quickly jotted a few sentences down. A few minutes later she cleared her throat. "Okay, everyone, listen to my literary masterpiece," she said. She began to read.

"'The Potato Bug,' by Stephanie Tanner. 'The potato bug was sitting on the leaf. Just hanging out. Sitting, sitting, sitting. Hanging, hanging, hanging.'"

"I liked 'it it it it it' better," said Michelle.

Stephanie nodded at her sister. "You're right. This story bites."

"No, no, I want to know more about this potato bug," said Danny. "What are his hobbies, his favorite color? What brand of fabric softener does he use?"

"How do I know?" said Stephanie. "He's a potato bug."

"Well, Stef," said Becky, "maybe you should write about what you *do* know—the people and things around you."

"Like what?" said Stephanie.

"You can write about *me*," said Michelle, pointing to herself with a periwinkle crayon.

"Or me," said Danny. "Write about what a cool dad you have."

Just then D.J. and Steve entered the kitchen. Kimmy was behind them.

"I can't believe you gave Kathy Santoni a ride home," D.J. was saying to Steve. Kathy Santoni was the head cheerleader at their high school—and one of the prettiest and most popular girls there.

"Hey, she had a tough day at cheerleading practice," Steve defended himself. "And she had a lot of stuff to carry home."

"But she lives next door to the school," D.J. reminded him.

"Ding!" said Kimmy, acting as the referee. "End of round six. So far, I've got this fight scored even." Suddenly she noticed the bowl of mashed potatoes. "What's this?" She stuck her finger in for a taste.

"Hey!" Michelle grabbed the bowl away.

"Not bad," Kimmy said, licking her lips. "What else is for supper, Pops?" she asked Danny.

"A home-cooked meal," Danny said, "so go home and start cooking." He led Kimmy to the door and ushered her out.

D.J. and Steve headed toward the living room.

"Kathy's such an airhead," D.J. was saying. "She signed up for *shop* class because she thought it was taught at the mall."

Suddenly Stephanie had an inspiration. She jumped up, grabbed her notebook, and raced after D.J. and Steve. What a great story idea, she thought. The main characters will be D.J. and Steve . . . no, P.J. and Cleve. It was better to use fake names so she wouldn't be found out. And she already had a perfect title: "The Young and the Jealous." This story would be the best thing she'd ever written. Things were beginning to brighten up after all.

FIVE

"Dad, is Steve here yet?" D.J. called from upstairs.

"No, but I am!" Kimmy yelled from the kitchen. She was sitting at the table eating breakfast with Stephanie and Michelle.

"Oh, hi, Kimmy," D.J. called. "Dad, would you let me know when Steve comes?" Then she closed her bedroom door.

Kimmy's smile faded. Stephanie watched her playing with the waffle on her plate. It looked like her appetite was gone too.

A few minutes later Stephanie and Michelle stood up.

"Wait up, little Tanners," Kimmy said. "I'll walk you to the corner."

Normally Stephanie would point out that she wasn't little. But today she felt sorry for her sister's best friend. It was obvious that Kimmy missed D.J. too.

Danny looked surprised. "Aren't you going to wait for D.J., Kimmy?" he asked.

Kimmy shrugged. "I just came over for the waffles," she said. "D.J. already has someone to walk to school with, and the two of them like to be alone." Suddenly her face brightened. "You know, I miss hanging out with D.J. now that she's going out with Steve, but I'm starting to develop other interests. In fact, I have this new activity after school—"

"Come on, Kimmy," Stephanie interrupted. "We're going to be late. You can tell us about it on the way."

As they left the house, Stephanie made a mental note to add a jealous friend named Pimmy to her story. Her story was getting better all the time.

A few minutes later D.J. opened her door again. "Dad, is Steve here yet?"

"No," said Danny. "But there are some waffles that are getting cold."

"Did I hear someone say 'waffles'?" said Steve cheerfully as he walked in through the kitchen door. "Hi, Mr. Tanner." He grabbed the last three slices of bacon from a plate and helped himself to two waffles.

"Steve's here now, Deej!" Danny announced.

D.J. hurried downstairs.

"Honey, you're finally wearing that blouse I got you," Danny said, smiling broadly. "I thought you hated that shade of blue."

"I do," D.J. said, picking up a banana, "but Steve loves it on me."

"Isn't it amazing the way it brings out her eyes?" Steve said, looking at D.J. adoringly.

"Maybe I'll buy her a matching skirt so she can have a whole outfit she hates," Danny commented sarcastically.

But Steve and D.J. were so busy gazing into each other's eyes that they didn't even hear him. With a sigh Danny began clearing plates from the table. "Oh, Deej, can you do me a favor?" he said.

"Sure, what is it, Dad?"

"Would you pick up Michelle from her Honeybees meeting at four o'clock? I want to be home when Vicky gets here. Her flight gets in from Chicago at three thirty."

"Michelle, Honeybees, four o'clock, got it," said D.J., still staring at Steve.

"Don't you think you ought to ask where the meeting is?" Danny suggested.

"Oh, yeah . . . right, Dad. Where is it?" said D.J.

Danny handed her a slip of paper with Michelle's friend Denise Patterson's address on it. "Don't forget—okay?"

"We'd better go, Deej," Steve said, grabbing another waffle for the road. "If I'm late for school too many times, they'll make me quit the wrestling team."

"Wait, D.J., weren't you supposed to get a history quiz back yesterday?" said Danny.

"Oh, yeah. I got a C," D.J. mumbled.

"All right! You nailed the test!" Steve said. He wasn't exactly a brilliant student.

"Hold it! You got a C?" said Danny. "D.J., you've always gotten A's in history. And we agreed that if you don't keep your grades up, you can't get a part-time job. And that means no saving up for that car you want."

"Oh, I don't need a car anymore. Steve has one." Before Danny could react, D.J. leaned over and gave him a kiss. "That should make you happy, Dad."

"Yeah," Steve jumped in eagerly. "I have this really cool car. It's a V-six, four on the floor, really roomy backseat . . ." His voice trailed off when he noticed the way Danny was looking at him.

"I don't know if I like the idea of you

driving D.J. around," Danny said. "She has two feet—she can walk or ride a bike."

"Dad!" D.J. cried. "Why are you being so difficult?"

"Uh . . . Deej," Steve mumbled, "I'll wait for you outside."

Danny turned to his daughter. "Look, Deej, I'm your father. I'm concerned about your schoolwork. I'm also concerned that you and Steve are getting too serious."

D.J. looked at Danny. "Steve is the best thing that ever happened to me."

Danny nodded. "I know you like him a lot. All I'm asking is that you remember what I said when I started giving you driving lessons."

"You mean, 'Pull over, I'm nauseous'?" said D.J.

Danny grinned. "Before that," he said. "I told you, 'Don't go too fast.'"

"Don't worry, Dad." D.J. patted him on the back. "We know what we're doing."

"I hope so," Danny mumbled as she left.

SIX

Stephanie crouched behind a book-case in a corner of the living room with her notebook in front of her. She had a great view of the couch, where D.J. and Steve were supposed to be doing geometry home-work. That was a joke, Stephanie thought. Steve may have come over to help D.J. with the subject, but her sister seemed to know a lot more about it than he did—not that it mattered. So far the two of them hadn't gotten anything accomplished. All D.J. wanted to do was discuss whether Steve had a crush on Kathy Santoni, the head cheerleader.

Now D.J. was playing with her hair. "Do you think Kathy Santoni's hair is bouncier than mine?" she asked in a pouty voice.

"Deej, I told you Kathy Santoni means nothing to me," Steve insisted. "Do you want to get some work done or not? Your dad's going to kill me if your grades drop."

"Okay, I'm sorry," D.J. apologized. "Let's get back to geometry."

"No, don't do that!" Stephanie wanted to shout. "The Young and the Jealous" was about to become "The Dull and the Boring"!

"To bisect the angle, put the tip of the compass here," said D.J.

Steve fumbled with the compass. "I can't get the hang of this, Deej."

She took his hand that was holding the compass needle and led him through the steps. "Put the needle here . . . and the pencil here . . ." Suddenly they were looking into each other's eyes.

"Who says geometry's a drag?" Steve whispered. They moved closer to each other, and just as they kissed, Becky and the twins burst through the front door.

"Uh-oh," said Nicky.

"Uh-oh," said Alex.

"Uh-oh is right," said Becky. "Nicky, Alex, this is what is known as bad timing. Excuse us. Passing through. We were never here, and now we're gone."

Stephanie held her breath as Becky hurried the twins along into the kitchen. Luckily none of them noticed Stephanie in her hiding spot.

The second D.J. and Steve were alone again, they started cooing at each other. After a few minutes of this, Stephanie wanted to vomit. Besides having to listen to all this disgusting talk, she wasn't getting anything good for her story. It was much more interesting when D.J. and Steve were arguing. Who knows when that will happen again, Stephanie thought, trying to shake a cramp out of her foot. At this rate, maybe never.

Unless . . . Stephanie tried to push the idea out of her head. But she had to do something. Her English assignment was due soon, and Steve had to leave in another hour. Besides, she told herself, this might be a way to get D.J. to stay home more often.

Her mind made up, Stephanie turned to a blank page in her notebook and began writing furiously.

A few minutes later, when Steve and D.J. went into the kitchen for a snack, Stephanie tore out the sheet of paper and slipped it into Steve's notebook. Then she tiptoed back to her hiding place behind the bookcase to watch and wait. . . .

SEVEN

"Okay, that's our last snack break," D.J. said to Steve as they returned to the living room.

Steve was carrying a big tray filled with M & M's, corn chips, oatmeal cookies, and a container of cheese spread.

Does this guy ever stop eating? Stephanie thought. No wonder Dad wants to get rid of him.

"I'm all set," said Steve. "We've got all

the basic food groups covered: salt, fat, sugar, and nacho cheese."

"Enough about food," said D.J., flipping the pages of her geometry book. "Okay, chapter two."

Steve opened his notebook. "What's this?" he said when he spotted the note Stephanie had left.

"'Dearest D.J.,'" he began reading aloud. "'I'll never forget our special kiss . . .'"

In her hiding place, Stephanie was writing as fast as she could.

D.J. leaned over to grab the note from Steve. "Let me see that," she demanded.

Steve held on tightly and continued: "'I'll never forget our special kiss in the lunchroom on macaroni day. Love, Henry.'" He turned to D.J. "Who's Henry?"

"I don't know a Henry," said D.J. "At least I don't think I do. . . ."

"Well, then who did you kiss on macaroni day?" Steve asked suspiciously.

"I didn't kiss anyone on macaroni day, or

on fish stick day, or on any other day," D.J. replied defensively.

"Yeah, right," said Steve. He stood up and shoved the note into his pocket. "Where's my jacket?" he asked. "I'm out of here."

"It's in my room," D.J. said. "But wait, Steve—this is a dumb joke or something." She followed him as he raced up the stairs to her room.

Stephanie started to go up after them. But as she scooped up her notebook and pen, her eye spotted the vent that was only a few feet away. It was the one that led to D.J.'s room. What a break, she thought. I'll be able to hear every word. In fact, she could even stretch out on the couch. Right now her feet were cramped and her back ached from having been crouched in such an uncomfortable position for so long.

"How could you do this to me?" Steve was saying. He sounded hurt.

"I didn't do anything to you," D.J. said. "You have to believe me."

"Why should I believe you?" Steve said. "The evidence is right there. You were caught red-handed, D.J."

"Steve," D.J. wailed. "Don't you trust me? My own boyfriend doesn't believe a word I say. That's just great—"

"How's the story going?"

Stephanie jumped. She'd been so busy listening and writing, she hadn't heard her dad come into the room.

"Oh . . . uh, hi, Dad. My story is . . . uh, really heating up," she replied brightly.

"That's great news, honey. May I read what you've got so far?" Danny asked, reaching for her notebook.

"Uh . . . now?" asked Stephanie. "It's not quite finished."

"That's okay, sweetheart. Vicky's plane was late, but she's due here from the airport at any minute. Maybe I can give you some pointers in the meantime."

Stephanie handed Danny the story. Luckily it had gotten quiet upstairs. She wasn't missing anything, and at least now Dad wouldn't be able to figure out that she'd been copying down every word D.J. and Steve said. "'Just when their love affair seemed peachy,'" Danny read, "'Cleve found a secret note of P.J.'s . . .'"

As Danny continued to read, Stephanie's nervousness faded. She was actually feeling kind of proud. Her story sounded great, and Danny didn't seem to have a clue that P.J. and Cleve were D.J. and Steve in real life.

Finally Danny came to the last lines that Stephanie had written. "'It was from Henry, her macaroni-day lover. Fireworks came shooting out of Cleve's ears and nose. . . .'"

"How's it sound?" Stephanie asked eagerly.

"Like Cleve needs a tissue," Danny joked. "I think it's very creative, Stef. It sounds just like a soap opera. I can't wait to find out what happens next."

"Thanks. I guess I'm just gifted," Stephanie couldn't resist bragging.

Suddenly they heard a door slam upstairs.

Then there was another slam.

"Is D.J. home already?" Danny looked concerned as he headed toward the stairs.

"Er . . . yeah, Dad," said Stephanie, thinking fast. "But she *really* wants to be alone, so I wouldn't bother her if I were you. And anyway, I wanted to tell you that the plant in the kitchen seemed kind of dusty before." Her father was a fanatic about keeping the house clean—Stephanie knew this would get him.

"How could that be?" asked Danny. "I dusted that plant yesterday—but I guess it can always use another going-over."

Stephanie heaved a sigh of relief as he left the room. A second later D.J. and Steve came back down the stairs. Steve had his jacket on and was heading for the front door.

"Steve, I'm telling you, the note is someone's idea of a joke," D.J. insisted. "I haven't kissed anyone but you."

But Steve was too angry to hear a word

D.J. said. He shook his fist in the air. "Just wait till I find out who this . . . this . . . noodlehead Henry is!" he exclaimed. Then he opened the front door and walked out, slamming it behind him.

With a sob, D.J. ran back upstairs.

EIGHT

D.J. flopped down onto her bed, planning to stay there for the rest of her life. Well, not *really* for the rest of her life—just until Steve would talk to her again, if he ever did. Who would have imagined that their relationship would end this way? she thought. Over a stupid note.

D.J. picked up the phone to call Kimmy but then hung up. She probably wasn't home. D.J. thought she remembered Kimmy saying that she'd become involved in some after-school activity. What could it be? D.J. wondered, feeling a pang of guilt. She hadn't been a very good friend to Kimmy lately. She'd been spending so much time with Steve that she hardly ever had time to see her best friend. In fact, the two of them hadn't even been to the mall together since they'd returned from Spain. And D.J. had been walking to school alone with Steve in the mornings and hanging out alone with him in the afternoons. Kimmy was probably mad at her. How could she expect Kimmy to be there for her now?

D.J.'s thoughts were interrupted by a knock on the door. Hoping it was Steve, she jumped off her bed, wiped her eyes, and ran a brush through her hair. But just as she was about to say "Come in," the door flew open and Michelle ran into the room.

"You forgot to pick me up from my Honeybees meeting," Michelle said accusingly.

"Can't I have any privacy? Haven't you

ever heard of knocking?" D.J. exclaimed.

"Haven't *you* ever heard of sticking to a promise?" Danny retorted angrily, coming in after Michelle. Vicky and Stephanie were behind him. "D.J., you *promised* me you'd pick up Michelle. When Stephanie told me you were home, I assumed Michelle was here, too. Denise Patterson's mother just dropped Michelle off."

D.J. gulped. "I'm really sorry, Dad."

"I'm not the only one you should be apologizing to," Danny said. D.J. had never seen him this angry before.

"Sorry, Michelle," D.J. mumbled. "Steve and I were really busy doing our homework."

"I've seen the way you do your homework when you're with Steve!" Danny snapped.

"Well, you won't get to see it anymore!" D.J. burst into tears.

Stephanie looked down. She felt terrible. It's all your fault, she told herself miserably.

Why did you have to write that letter?

Danny turned to Vicky. "Sorry about this, honey," he said. "You must be starving. Girls, can you take Vicky down to the kitchen and get her something to eat? I want to talk to D.J. alone."

"I never get to see the good stuff," Michelle complained as the three of them left the room. But Stephanie was secretly relieved to have an excuse to get out of there.

The last thing she wanted to do was hear more about how she'd ruined her sister's life.

When D.J. was alone with her dad, she sat on her bed. She looked at Danny.

"D.J., forgetting to pick up Michelle was inexcusable," Danny said.

"I know, Dad. You've already told me that. I promise it'll never happen again," she answered.

"It's not just forgetting Michelle," Danny said. "You're too wrapped up with Steve."

D.J.'s eyes filled with tears again. Her dad didn't understand at all how she felt about

Steve—and now it was all over. "I love him," she mumbled.

"What?" Danny exclaimed. "You're not in love. You're only sixteen. And right now your head is in the clouds. You haven't been paying attention to your schoolwork, and you've been neglecting all your responsibilities."

"I *said* I was sorry." D.J. wished her father would just leave her to her own misery.

"I'm sorry, too, D.J., because I don't want you and Steve seeing each other for a month," Danny said sternly.

"You can't make rules like that!" D.J. said, jumping up from her bed.

"I just did," Danny replied.

Her dad was being so unfair. If Steve would take her back, she'd be his in a second—no matter what her dad said. D.J. ran downstairs and out the front door.

"D.J.!" Danny called after her. "D.J.!"

But she was gone.

NINE

D.J. slammed the front door so hard that the entire house shook. Joey came running up from the basement screaming "Earthquake!" Jesse came in from the garage, where he'd been polishing his motorcycle. Becky came downstairs with a twin in each arm, looking bewildered. And Stephanie, Michelle, and Vicky came running from the kitchen into the living room.

Danny stood there looking lost. "D.J.

just took off," he explained. "We had an argument about Steve, and then she left."

"Where'd she go?" Michelle asked.

"I don't know, honey," Danny said. He looked at the others. "Any ideas?"

"Well," said Vicky, "my first guess would be Steve's house."

"I'm sure you're right," said Danny. "Does anyone know where to find him?"

"He's taking a nap," Michelle said.

"What?" Everyone looked at her.

"He's at resting practice," she explained.

"I think she means *wrestling* practice," said Jesse, "and Michelle is right. He's probably at the school gym."

Stephanie opened her mouth to speak. She wanted to tell her dad that D.J. and Steve had just had a fight and that maybe D.J. wouldn't try to find him. But no words came out. Things had gotten so complicated so fast—and it was all her fault.

Danny grabbed his jacket and car keys. "Then that's where I'm going." He looked at Vicky. "I'm afraid you came all the way from Chicago to watch me go on a daughter chase."

"Don't worry," Vicky said. She smiled at Stephanie and Michelle. "I'm in good company."

"Thanks," Danny said. He blew her a kiss and left the house. Becky took the twins back upstairs, and Jesse turned to Joey.

"C'mon," he said. "Let's start dinner."

"First, can someone please tell me why D.J. left," said Joey.

"I don't know," said Jesse, "but I have a feeling she'll need some cheering up. Let's make her favorite dinner."

"Spaghetti it is." Joey followed Jesse to the kitchen.

"Vicky, want to come up to my room to play with Pigaro and Eduardo?" Michelle asked.

"Sure," Vicky replied. "Come on, Stephanie."

Stephanie shook her head. "I think I'll

stay here and work on my story for English," she said. But the truth was that she wasn't feeling very well and she wanted to be alone to think. If only she could patch things up between D.J. and Steve. If only she'd been able to tell Danny the truth. If only this whole thing had never happened.

TEN

Wrestling practice was almost over when Danny walked into the school gym. Rubber mats were spread out all over the shiny wooden floor, and each one had a pair of wrestlers on it. Lots of grunting and groaning was going on, and the place smelled of sweat and dirty feet.

The coach was standing at the opposite end of the gym, showing a headlock hold to one pair of wrestlers.

"Hey, Coach, telephone!" said a familiar voice.

Danny turned around and saw Kimmy Gibbler. Kimmy was wearing a green sweatsuit and carrying a stack of clean towels.

"Gibbler, what are you doing here?" Danny asked.

"Hi, Mr. T.," Kimmy said. "You're looking at the new wrestling team towel girl."

"When did you get *this* job?" Danny asked.

"I've had some free time lately," Kimmy explained. "And this seemed like a good way to help my school."

"Oh, really," Danny said as he looked around the gym. "Have you seen D.J.?"

Kimmy shook her head. "No. Why would she be here?"

"I don't have time to explain right now," Danny replied. "Do you know where Steve is?"

"Sure do," Kimmy said. She led Danny over to a mat in a corner of the room. Sure enough, Steve was there, pinned under his 230-pound opponent.

"Steve, where's D.J.?" Danny demanded.

"I haven't seen her . . . since . . ." Steve panted as he struggled to free himself from the other wrestler's hold.

"I don't have all day," Danny said impatiently.

"Since I left your house . . . this afternoon," Steve said.

"Well, she's disappeared," Danny said.

Steve looked startled. "Oh, man, she must really . . . be freaked," he managed to get out.

"Steve, I need your help," Danny said. "You really care about D.J., don't you?"

"I love her, Mr. Tanner," Steve said. "I just don't . . . know . . . if she loves me."

"I wish you kids would stop using that love word," replied Danny.

"Look, Mr. Tanner . . . I've got to . . . practice or Coach is going to flip out," Steve said. He focused on his wrestling partner.

Danny bent down and tapped Steve's husky opponent on the shoulder. "Take five, killer," he said.

Grunting, the boy got up. Danny immediately took his place, pinning Steve down.

"Mr. Tanner, why are you on top of me?" Steve asked.

"*You* need to wrestle. *I* need to talk."

"Mr. Tanner, you're old. Your bones are brittle."

"Don't worry about my bones," Danny said. "They called me the Steel String Bean at school."

"I buy the string bean part," Kimmy chimed in.

"Just give us the cue to start, Kimmy," Danny said.

"You mean 'Ready, wrestle'?" Kimmy said. And just as she said it, Steve took Danny off guard and shot up, flipping him onto his back. Some of the other wrestlers gathered around to watch.

Danny grunted. This wrestling stuff

looked a lot easier than it actually was. "Steve, since you and D.J. started dating, her grades have been going down." He took a few deep breaths. "I'm sure your wrestling must be suffering too."

"Actually, she inspires me, Mr. Tanner," Steve said. "My wrestling has never been better." He tightened his hold on Danny as if to show him.

"Think about your parents, Steve," Danny went on. "Aren't they concerned that you're spending so much time with D.J.?"

While Steve was thinking about how he would answer that, Danny scrambled free.

"Escape!" called Kimmy. "One point for the Bean of Steel."

Both Danny and Steve got to their feet. They circled each other.

"My parents think D.J.'s the greatest girl in the world," Steve said. "And so do I— even if she does like the macaroni man better than me."

"Who?" Danny said.

"The macaroni man," replied Steve.

"Are you talking about *Henry,* the macaroni man?" Danny quickly moved in to grasp Steve around the waist and flip him onto the mat. He pinned Steve.

Steve was stunned. "You know Henry? Who is he?"

"Dad!" D.J. suddenly shrieked. "What are you doing? Leave Steve alone!"

As soon as Steve realized that D.J. was there, he broke free of Danny's hold. "It's all right, D.J.," he said, getting to his feet. "Your father was just helping me practice."

D.J. was looking from her father to Steve to Kimmy. On her face was an expression of utter confusion. "I don't get it. What are all of you doing here?" she asked. "Kimmy, your mom told me I'd find you at school, but I had no idea you were part of the wrestling team!"

Kimmy shrugged. "You've been so busy . . ." she said. "I got tired of hanging out alone all the time. Then I remembered that

Steve had said the wrestling team needed some help. And where there are cute guys, I'm always willing to lend a helping hand."

"I'm sorry, Kimmy," D.J. said softly. "I know I haven't been around much." She glanced at Steve. "All Steve and I want to do is be alone together—well, that's the way we *used* to feel, anyway."

Steve looked down.

"You have to believe me, Steve," D.J. said. "I'm not sure why, but someone wrote that note to get me in trouble with you."

"I want to believe you, Deej," Steve replied. "I just don't know about this macaroni man. . . ."

Note . . . macaroni man . . . Danny listened in silence. Why were Steve and D.J. talking about details from Stephanie's short story? Then something clicked in his brain, and the pieces fell into place. "Uh, D.J., Steve," Danny began. He wasn't too happy about D.J. and Steve spending so much time together, but he couldn't let them break up over this. "Have you read Stephanie's story for English class?"

D.J. looked at him. Why was he talking about Stephanie's school assignment at a time like this? "No . . ." she said.

"You should take a look at it," Danny went on. "It might help to explain a few things."

ELEVEN

"This is incredible!" said D.J. as she and Steve read Stephanie's story. "'Cleve found a secret note of P.J.'s. It was from Henry, her macaroni-day lover.'"

"Yeah." Steve looked amazed. "The same thing happened to us."

D.J. looked at her father and shrugged. Okay, so Steve wasn't the smartest boyfriend in the world.

Danny had driven D.J. and Steve from the

gym to the Tanners' house. They'd found Stephanie's notebook in a pile with her schoolbooks by the bookcase in the living room.

"So, Steve," said D.J., "do you forgive me now?"

Steve was lost in his own thoughts. "I see," he finally said. "Stephanie wrote the note so *I* would get jealous in real life, and she could write about it in a story."

"Exactly," said D.J.

"Well, for a joke," commented Steve, "it wasn't too funny."

"Stephanie has to learn the difference between a story and real life," Danny said.

"I don't think she should get away with this," said D.J. "We have to think of a way to get back at her."

"Whoa, Deej," said Danny. "Maybe I should just go up and talk to her."

"Please, Dad," D.J. pleaded. "I just need a little revenge." She thought a moment. "Wait a second. I've got it." She smiled mischievously and then filled Danny and Steve in on her plan.

"Spaghetti's ready," Joey called from the kitchen. He came into the living room. "Welcome back, D.J. Hi, Steve."

"Hi, Joey," Steve said.

"Do you want to stay for dinner, Steve?" D.J. asked.

Danny was relieved to see Steve shake his head.

"I think I'll eat at home for a change, Deej," he said. "My mom's making my favorite dish—macaroni and cheese. Actually, I think I'll just have the cheese part of it tonight. I've had enough macaroni for a while."

D.J. grinned. "Hey, Dad, see that dust ball?" She pointed toward the floor. As soon as Danny bent down, D.J. wrapped her arms around Steve and kissed him.

"I don't see a dust ball," Danny said. When he looked up, Steve was gone.

TWELVE

After school the next day, Stephanie sat at the kitchen table working on "The Young and the Jealous." Her story was due the next day, and she still hadn't finished. She was glad that D.J. and Steve had made up and D.J. was happy again, but there was a small piece of her that was disappointed too. Now she was stuck making up an ending for her story, and she didn't have any ideas at all.

D.J. and Steve walked into the kitchen holding hands. They seemed not to see Stephanie.

"You know, Steve," D.J. was saying, "in a way the argument we had over that note is the best thing that ever happened to us."

Stephanie glanced up. *What?*

"I know, sweetheart," Steve said. "Just thinking about you kissing another guy on macaroni day has made me realize so many things. We can't go on like this." He dropped to one knee, still holding D.J.'s hand. "Let's get married."

Stephanie's mouth dropped open.

"Oh, Steve," D.J. purred. "What a wonderful idea. I can't wait another minute— let's do it tomorrow. There's only half a day of school."

Steve embraced her. "Perfect," he murmured.

Oh, no, Stephanie thought. What have I done? They're too young to get married— D.J. is making a big mistake!

"Hi, everyone," Danny said as he entered the room.

"Dad," said D.J. "We have to talk."

"That's what dads are for," Danny said.

Stephanie was speechless. She couldn't believe that D.J. was going to tell her dad that she was going to get married. Her dad was going to flip out!

"Mr. Tanner, sir . . . uh, Dad," said Steve. "I want to marry your daughter."

Danny shot out of his chair. "What?" he cried. "You've been dating since the summer!" He clapped Steve on the back. "What took you so long, son?" He gave D.J. a hug.

Stephanie was in shock. "Dad, you can't be serious."

"Why not, honey?" said Danny. "D.J. and Steve can live right here with us. They can take your room, and Michelle can take D.J.'s room."

"But where am I going to sleep?" asked Stephanie.

"Oh, yeah. I forgot about you." Danny

pretended to think for a moment. "How about the laundry room?"

"That's where the dog sleeps!" Stephanie replied.

"Great," said Danny. "You and Comet can keep each other warm."

"Dad, you can't do this to me," Stephanie pleaded. "And you can't let D.J. and Steve get married. She's only sixteen."

"Why can't we get married?" asked D.J. "It will make a great ending to your story."

"My story?" Stephanie echoed weakly.

D.J., Steve, and Danny were all staring. Stephanie forced a little laugh. "You guys read my story? So what do you think?"

"I think you did a pretty rotten thing, Stephanie Judith Tanner," said Danny. "You can't disrupt people's lives like that."

"I didn't mean to hurt anybody," Stephanie said. "I felt terrible when D.J. and Steve had the fight." She looked at D.J. "I was going to tell you I wrote the note when you came home, but you and Steve had already made up. Can you guys forgive me?" she added softly.

"Uh—" Steve said.

"Don't make it easy for her, Steve," D.J. interrupted. "She almost broke us up for good." She shot Stephanie an angry look.

"D.J., don't you think you're being just a little bit hard on your sister?" Danny said.

"No!" D.J. said stubbornly.

"Okay," Stephanie said. "How's this: Steve, if you forgive me, I'll get Dad to make you his special corn dogs." She knew that Steve loved Dad's corn dogs. Actually, he loved everything that Dad made, but corn dogs seemed to be a special favorite.

"Cool!" Steve replied.

Stephanie smiled and looked at D.J. Now that Steve had accepted her apology, it wouldn't be long until D.J. did too.

But D.J. wasn't about to let Stephanie off the hook so easily.

"If I agree to forgive you," said D.J., "you have to clean my room for a week."

"Okay," said Stephanie. That wasn't *too* bad.

But D.J. wasn't finished. "And clear the dinner dishes instead of me. And walk the dog after school. And . . . well, I'm sure I'll think of more things later."

Stephanie sighed and nodded.

THIRTEEN

That night D.J. was just hanging up the phone in her room when Danny knocked, then entered. As usual, she'd been talking to Steve.

"I want to discuss your relationship with Steve," said Danny.

"If you're going to tell me again that we can't see each other for a while, then I don't think you're being fair," said D.J. "You don't know how terrible I felt when Steve was mad and wouldn't talk to me."

"Actually, Deej, I'm not going to tell you that you can't see Steve," Danny responded. He sat on the bed. "Just the opposite."

"What do you mean?" D.J. asked.

Her father paused, then said, "I told Vicky I loved her today."

"You did?" said D.J., looking interested.

"Yes, I did," said Danny. "I haven't been in love with anyone since your mom—and it feels incredible."

"That's great, Dad," D.J. said.

"It is," Danny said, "and it made me think about how you and Steve must feel about each other. If you and Steve are feeling the way I am, I think it's wonderful."

"Are you saying I can see Steve as much as I want to?" D.J. said, brightening a little.

"No." Danny shook his head. "I want you to keep your grades up. But I will let you see enough of him." He gave his daughter a big hug. "The truth is, Steve's a nice kid. He's polite, he cares a lot about you, he's a good eater, and he has a heck of a headlock." Danny rubbed his neck.

"Thanks, Dad," D.J. said. "I can't wait to call him back and tell him!" She picked up the phone.

"Whoa, let's put that call on hold for a minute," Danny said. "When was the last time you and Stephanie hung out together?" he asked. "And when was the last time you read to Michelle?"

D.J. stared at her comforter. She knew she hadn't had much time for Stephanie since she'd returned from Spain. She'd also been neglecting Michelle. A blush washed over her face as she remembered how she'd forgotten to pick up her little sister from the Honeybees meeting. Being with Steve was the most exciting thing that had ever happened to her, but she'd let it take over her whole world.

"I don't think I've done anything with either one of them since I got back from Spain," she mumbled.

Danny didn't say anything. He just nodded.

"I get your point, Dad," D.J. said. She stood up. "I'm going in to talk to both of them right now."

Danny smiled and gave her a thumbs-up.

FOURTEEN

Stephanie was sitting on her bed waiting for her nails to dry. The Perfect Pink nail polish she was using had been a birthday present from D.J. This year D.J. probably won't even give me anything, Stephanie thought ruefully. I'll bet this is the last present I get from her for the next fifty years. Maybe she'll finally talk to me when she's on her deathbed or something.

From the opposite bed, Michelle was

watching Stephanie wave her wet fingernails in the air. "Is D.J. going to marry Steve?" she asked.

"Maybe someday," Stephanie said, "but not in the near future—at least I hope not."

"Me too," Michelle said. "She still has to read all those books to me." She pointed to a pile of books on her work table.

"I can read to you, Michelle," Stephanie said.

"But D.J. makes the best animal noises," Michelle said. Stephanie couldn't argue with that.

There was a knock on the door.

"Who is it?" Michelle called.

"D.J."

"D.J. who?" asked Michelle.

"D.J., your sister."

"D.J., your sister, who?" Michelle said.

"Come in, Deej," Stephanie interrupted.

"Hey, you guys," D.J. said as she stepped into the room. "I feel like I haven't talked to you in the longest time."

"You can say that again," Stephanie said.

"Listen, I forgive you for writing that story, and I'm sorry I haven't been around much," D.J. went on. "It's just that . . ."

"We know," said Michelle. "You have a boyfriend now."

"That's true," said D.J., "but—"

"Look, D.J.," Stephanie said, "I had a crummy summer, and then you came back and didn't even care about me or Michelle. You just brought us stuffed animals, which *I* happen to have outgrown."

"Sorry, Stef. I should have realized that," D.J. said.

"I like Pigaro and Eduardo." Michelle picked up the pig and the mouse and hugged them.

D.J. turned to Stephanie. "What did you mean when you said I didn't care about you?" she asked.

"You were too busy kissing Steve," Michelle put in.

"Yeah," Stephanie chimed in. "You never

want to do anything with us anymore."

"Just because I have a boyfriend now doesn't mean that I don't care about you two," D.J. said. "When I was in Spain, I missed you both like crazy."

"You did?" Stephanie said.

"Of course," D.J. said. "Didn't you read my postcards?" She sat down on Stephanie's bed. "Look, a lot of things changed for me this summer, but there's one thing that will never change: that's how much I love you two."

"But what if you marry Steve and have ten children and two dogs, and a horse . . ." Stephanie's voice trailed off.

"Stef, Stef . . . trust me, I'll love you." D.J. sounded as if she meant it. "Oh, I almost forgot," she went on. "Steve's cousin is going to be in town this weekend, and he's your age, Stef. Steve wants to know if you want to go out, the four of us."

"Sure!" answered Stephanie, glad that she had just polished her nails. This would be great. It would be just like a real date!

"I want to go too," Michelle said. "Tell him to bring a cousin who's *my* age."

"Steve doesn't have a cousin who is your age, Michelle," D.J. said. "But there will be other times that you can go out with us."

"Okay," Michelle said, looking sad. Then she brightened. "D.J., can you read me a story?"

D.J. smiled and rumpled Michelle's hair. "Sure. But you'll have to wait a minute. I have a phone call to make."

Stephanie groaned. "You're not going to call Steve again!"

D.J. shook her head. "Nope. I'm calling Kimmy. We need to make a date for some shopping at the mall."

"Hey, Deej," Stephanie said. "Before you read to Michelle, could you do something for me, too?"

D.J. beamed at Stephanie. She was glad that things between them were finally back to normal. "Anything," she replied.

"Could you help me finish my story?" Stephanie asked sweetly.

She barely managed to duck out of the way as D.J. fired a pillow directly at her head.

"Sisters!" D.J. said. "You have to love 'em!"